PENGUIN BOOKS

A Very Old Man with Enormous Wings

'Márquez writes in this lyrical, magical language that no one else can do' Salman Rushdie

'Of all the living authors known to me, only one is undoubtedly touched by genius: Gabriel García Márquez' *Sunday Telegraph*

'The most important writer of fiction in any language' Bill Clinton

'An imaginative writer of genius, the topmost pinnacle of an entire generation of Latin American novelists of cathedral-like proportions' *Guardian*

'One of this century's most evocative writers' Anne Tyler

'Márquez is a retailer of wonders' *Sunday Times*

'Sentence for sentence, there is hardly another writer in the world so generous with incidental pleasures' *Independent*

CW00820237

ABOUT THE AUTHOR

Gabriel García Márquez was born in Aracataca, Colombia, in 1927. He studied at the University of Botoga and later worked as a reporter for the Colombian newspaper *El Espectador* and as a foreign correspondent in Rome, Paris, Barcelona, Caracas and New York. He is the author of several novels and collections of stories, including *Eyes of a Blue Dog* (1947), *Leaf Storm* (1955), *No One Writes to the Colonel* (1958), *In Evil Hour* (1962), *Big Mama's Funeral* (1962), *One Hundred Years of Solitude* (1967), *Innocent Erendira and Other Stories* (1972), *The Autumn of the Patriarch* (1975), *Chronicle of a Death Foretold* (1981), *Love in the Time of Cholera* (1985), *The General in His Labyrinth* (1989), *Strange Pilgrims* (1992), *Of Love and Other Demons* (1994) and *Memories of My Melancholy Whores* (2005). Many of his books are published by Penguin. Gabriel García Márquez was awarded the Nobel Prize for Literature in 1982. He lives in Mexico City.

Gabriel García Márquez

A Very Old Man with Enormous Wings
and
The Sea of Lost Time

Translated from the Spanish by
Gregory Rabassa

PENGUIN BOOKS

PENGUIN BOOKS

Published by the Penguin Group
Penguin Books Ltd, 80 Strand, London WC2R ORL, England
Penguin Group (USA) Inc., 375 Hudson Street, New York, New York 10014, USA
Penguin Group (Canada), 90 Eglinton Avenue East, Suite 700, Toronto,
Ontario, Canada M4P 2Y3
(a division of Pearson Penguin Canada Inc.)
Penguin Ireland, 25 St Stephen's Green, Dublin 2, Ireland (a division of Penguin Books Ltd)
Penguin Group (Australia), 707 Collins Street, Melbourne, Victoria 3008, Australia
(a division of Pearson Australia Group Pty Ltd)
Penguin Books India Pvt Ltd, 11 Community Centre, Panchsheel Park,
New Delhi – 110 017, India
Penguin Group (NZ), 67 Apollo Drive, Rosedale, Auckland 0632, New Zealand
(a division of Pearson New Zealand Ltd)
Penguin Books (South Africa) (Pty) Ltd, Block D, Rosebank Office Park,
181 Jan Smuts Avenue, Parktown North, Gauteng 2193, South Africa

Penguin Books Ltd, Registered Offices: 80 Strand, London WC2R ORL, England

www.penguin.com

'A Very Old Man with Enormous Wings' first appeared in *New American Review*;
'The Sea of Lost Time' in the *New Yorker*
First published as part of a collection by Jonathan Cape 1991
First published in *Collected Stories* in Penguin Books 1996
This collection first published in Penguin Books 2014

002

Copyright © Gabriel García Márquez, 1954, 1961
English translations copyright © Harper & Row Publishers, Inc., 1978
All rights reserved

The moral right of the copyright holders has been asserted

Printed in Great Britain by Clays Ltd, St Ives plc

ISBN: 978-0-241-96958-8

www.greenpenguin.co.uk

MIX
Paper from
responsible sources
FSC® C018179
www.fsc.org

Penguin Books is committed to a sustainable
future for our business, our readers and our planet.
This book is made from Forest Stewardship
Council™ certified paper.

A Very Old Man
with Enormous Wings

A TALE FOR CHILDREN

On the third day of rain they had killed so many crabs inside the house that Pelayo had to cross his drenched courtyard and throw them into the sea, because the newborn child had a temperature all night and they thought it was due to the stench. The world had been sad since Tuesday. Sea and sky were a single ash-gray thing and the sands of the beach, which on March nights glimmered like powdered light, had become a stew of mud and rotten shellfish. The light was so weak at noon that when Pelayo was coming back to the house after throwing away the crabs, it was hard for him to see what it was that was moving and groaning in the rear of the courtyard. He had to go very close to see that it was an old man, lying face down in the mud, who, in spite of his tremendous efforts, couldn't get up, impeded by his enormous wings.

Frightened by that nightmare, Pelayo ran to get Elisenda, his wife, who was putting compresses on the sick child, and he took her to the rear of the courtyard. They both looked at the fallen body with mute stupor. He was dressed like a ragpicker. There were only a few faded hairs left on his bald skull and very few teeth in his mouth, and his pitiful condition of a drenched great-grandfather had taken away any sense of grandeur he might have had. His huge buzzard wings, dirty and half-plucked, were forever entangled in the mud. They looked at him so long and so closely that Pelayo and Elisenda very soon overcame their surprise and in the end found him familiar. Then they dared speak to him, and he answered in an incomprehensible dialect with a strong sailor's voice. That was how they skipped over the inconvenience of the wings and quite intelligently concluded that he was a lonely castaway from some foreign ship wrecked by the storm. And yet, they called in a neighbor woman who knew everything about life and death to see him, and all she needed was one look to show them their mistake.

'He's an angel,' she told them. 'He must have been coming for the child, but the poor fellow is so old that the rain knocked him down.'

On the following day everyone knew that a flesh-and-blood angel was held captive in Pelayo's house. Against the judgment of the wise neighbor woman, for whom angels in those times were the fugitive survivors of a celestial conspiracy, they did not have the heart to club him to death. Pelayo watched over him all afternoon from the kitchen, armed with his bailiff's club, and before going to bed he dragged him out of the mud and locked him up with the hens in the wire chicken coop. In the middle of the night, when the rain stopped, Pelayo and Elisenda were still killing crabs. A short time afterward the child woke up without a fever and with a desire to eat. Then they felt magnanimous and decided to put the angel on a raft with fresh water and provisions for three days and leave him to his fate on the high seas. But when they went out into the courtyard with the first light of dawn, they found the whole neighborhood in front of the chicken coop having fun with the angel, without the slightest reverence, tossing him things to eat through the openings in the wire as if he weren't a supernatural creature but a circus animal.

Father Gonzaga arrived before seven o'clock, alarmed at the strange news. By that time onlookers less frivolous than those at dawn had already arrived and they were making all kinds of conjectures concerning the captive's future. The simplest among them thought that he should be named mayor of the world. Others of sterner mind felt that he should be promoted to the rank of five-star general in order to win all wars. Some visionaries hoped that he could be put to stud in order to implant on earth a race of winged wise men who could take charge of the universe. But Father Gonzaga, before becoming a priest, had been a robust woodcutter. Standing by the wire, he reviewed his catechism in an instant and asked them to open the door so that he could take a close look at that pitiful man who looked more like a huge decrepit hen among the fascinated chickens. He was lying in a corner drying his open wings in the sunlight among the fruit peels and breakfast leftovers that the early risers had thrown him. Alien to the impertinences of the world, he only lifted his antiquarian eyes and murmured something in his dialect when Father Gonzaga went into the chicken coop and said good morning to him in Latin. The parish priest had his first suspicion of an imposter when he saw that he did not understand the language of God or know how to greet His ministers. Then he noticed that seen close up he was much too human: he had an unbearable smell of the outdoors, the back side of his wings was strewn with parasites and his main feathers had been mistreated by terrestrial winds, and nothing about him measured up to the proud dignity of angels. Then he came out of the chicken coop and in a brief sermon warned the curious against the risks of being ingenuous. He reminded them that the devil had the bad habit of making use of carnival tricks in order to confuse the unwary. He argued that if wings were not the essential element in determining the difference between a hawk and an airplane, they were even less so in the recognition of angels. Nevertheless, he promised to write a letter to his bishop so that the latter would write to his primate so that the latter would write to the Supreme Pontiff in order to get the final verdict from the highest courts.

His prudence fell on sterile hearts. The news of the captive angel spread with such rapidity that after a few hours the courtyard had the bustle of a marketplace and they had to call in troops with fixed bayonets to disperse the mob that was about to knock the house down. Elisenda, her spine all twisted from sweeping up so much marketplace trash, then got the idea of fencing in the yard and charging five cents admission to see the angel.

The curious came from far away. A traveling carnival arrived with a flying acrobat who buzzed over the crowd several times, but no one paid any attention to him because his wings were not those of an angel but, rather, those of a sidereal bat. The most unfortunate invalids on earth came in search of health: a poor woman who since childhood had been counting her heartbeats and had run out of numbers; a Portuguese man who couldn't sleep because the noise of the stars disturbed him; a sleepwalker who got up at night to undo the things he had done while awake; and many others with less serious ailments. In the midst of that shipwreck disorder that made the earth tremble, Pelayo and Elisenda were happy with fatigue, for in less than a week they had crammed their rooms with money and the line of pilgrims waiting their turn to enter still reached beyond the horizon.

The angel was the only one who took no part in his own act. He spent his time trying to get comfortable in his borrowed nest, befuddled by the hellish heat of the oil lamps and sacramental candles that had been placed along the wire. At first they tried to make him eat some mothballs, which, according to the wisdom of the wise neighbor woman, were the food prescribed for angels. But he turned them down, just as he turned down the papal lunches that the penitents brought him, and they never found out whether it was because he was an angel or because he was an old man that in the end he ate nothing but eggplant mush. His only supernatural virtue seemed to be patience. Especially during the first days, when the hens pecked at him, searching for the stellar parasites that proliferated in his wings, and the cripples pulled out feathers to touch their defective parts with, and even the most merciful threw stones at him, trying to get him to rise so they could see him standing. The only time they succeeded in arousing him was when they burned his side with an iron for branding steers, for he had been motionless for so many hours that they thought he was dead. He awoke with a start, ranting in his hermetic language and with tears in his eyes, and he flapped his wings a couple of times, which brought on a

whirlwind of chicken dung and lunar dust and a gale of panic
that did not seem to be of this world. Although many thought
that his reaction had been one not of rage but of pain, from
then on they were careful not to annoy him, because the
majority understood that his passivity was not that of a hero
taking his ease but that of a cataclysm in repose.

Father Gonzaga held back the crowd's frivolity with formu-
las of maidservant inspiration while awaiting the arrival of a
final judgment on the nature of the captive. But the mail from
Rome showed no sense of urgency. They spent their time
finding out if the prisoner had a navel, if his dialect had any
connection with Aramaic, how many times he could fit on the
head of a pin, or whether he wasn't just a Norwegian with
wings. Those meager letters might have come and gone until
the end of time if a providential event had not put an end to
the priest's tribulations.

It so happened that during those days, among so many
other carnival attractions, there arrived in town the traveling
show of the woman who had been changed into a spider for
having disobeyed her parents. The admission to see her was
not only less than the admission to see the angel, but people
were permitted to ask her all manner of questions about her
absurd state and to examine her up and down so that no one
would ever doubt the truth of her horror. She was a frightful
tarantula the size of a ram and with the head of a sad maiden.
What was most heartrending, however, was not her out-
landish shape but the sincere affliction with which she re-
counted the details of her misfortune. While still practically a
child she had sneaked out of her parents' house to go to a
dance, and while she was coming back through the woods
after having danced all night without permission, a fearful
thunderclap rent the sky in two and through the crack came
the lightning bolt of brimstone that changed her into a spider.
Her only nourishment came from the meatballs that charitable souls chose to toss into her mouth. A spectacle like that,
full of so much human truth and with such a fearful lesson,
was bound to defeat without even trying that of a haughty

angel who scarcely deigned to look at mortals. Besides, the few miracles attributed to the angel showed a certain mental disorder, like the blind man who didn't recover his sight but grew three new teeth, or the paralytic who didn't get to walk but almost won the lottery, and the leper whose sores sprouted sunflowers. Those consolation miracles, which were more like mocking fun, had already ruined the angel's reputation when the woman who had been changed into a spider finally crushed him completely. That was how Father Gonzaga was cured forever of his insomnia and Pelayo's courtyard went back to being as empty as during the time it had rained for three days and crabs walked through the bedrooms.

The owners of the house had no reason to lament. With the money they saved they built a two-story mansion with balconies and gardens and high netting so that crabs wouldn't get in during the winter, and with iron bars on the windows so that angels wouldn't get in. Pelayo also set up a rabbit warren close to town and gave up his job as bailiff for good, and Elisenda bought some satin pumps with high heels and many dresses of iridescent silk, the kind worn on Sunday by the most desirable women in those times. The chicken coop was the only thing that didn't receive any attention. If they washed it down with creolin and burned tears of myrrh inside it every so often, it was not in homage to the angel but to drive away the dungheap stench that still hung everywhere like a ghost and was turning the new house into an old one. At first, when the child learned to walk, they were careful that he did not get too close to the chicken coop. But then they began to lose their fears and got used to the smell, and before the child got his second teeth he'd gone inside the chicken coop to play, where the wires were falling apart. The angel was no less standoffish with him than with other mortals, but he tolerated the most ingenious infamies with the patience of a dog who had no illusions. They both came down with chicken-pox at the same time. The doctor who took care of the child couldn't resist the temptation to listen to the angel's heart, and he found so much whistling in the heart and so many sounds in his kidneys that it seemed impossible for him to be alive. What surprised him most, however, was the logic of his wings. They seemed so natural on that completely human organism that he couldn't understand why other men didn't have them too.

When the child began school it had been some time since the sun and rain had caused the collapse of the chicken coop. The angel went dragging himself about here and there like a stray dying man. They would drive him out of the bedroom with a broom and a moment later find him in the kitchen. He seemed to be in so many places at the same time that they grew to think that he'd been duplicated, that he was reproducing himself all through the house, and the exasperated and unhinged Elisenda shouted that it was awful living in that hell full of angels. He could scarcely eat and his antiquarian eyes had also become so foggy that he went about bumping into posts. All he had left were the bare cannulae of his last feathers. Pelayo threw a blanket over him and extended him the charity of letting him sleep in the shed, and only then did they notice that he had a temperature at night, and was delirious with the tongue twisters of an old Norwegian. That was one of the few times they became alarmed, for they thought he was going to die and not even the wise neighbor woman had been able to tell them what to do with dead angels.

And yet he not only survived his worst winter, but seemed improved with the first sunny days. He remained motionless for several days in the farthest corner of the courtyard, where no one would see him, and at the beginning of December some large, stiff feathers began to grow on his wings, the feathers of a scarecrow, which looked more like another misfortune of decrepitude. But he must have known the reason for those changes, for he was quite careful that no one should notice them, that no one should hear the sea chanteys that he sometimes sang under the stars. One morning Elisenda was cutting some bunches of onions for lunch when a wind that seemed to come from the high seas blew into the kitchen.

Gabriel García Márquez

Then she went to the window and caught the angel in his first attempts at flight. They were so clumsy that his fingernails opened a furrow in the vegetable patch and he was on the point of knocking the shed down with the ungainly flapping that slipped on the light and couldn't get a grip on the air. But he did manage to gain altitude. Elisenda let out a sigh of relief, for herself and for him, when she saw him pass over the last houses, holding himself up in some way with the risky flapping of a senile vulture. She kept watching him even when she was through cutting the onions and she kept on watching until it was no longer possible for her to see him, because then he was no longer an annoyance in her life but an imaginary dot on the horizon of the sea.

The Sea of Lost Time

Toward the end of January the sea was growing harsh, it was beginning to dump its heavy garbage on the town, and a few weeks later everything was contaminated with its unbearable mood. From that time on the world wasn't worth living in, at least until the following December, so no one stayed awake after eight o'clock. But the year Mr Herbert came the sea didn't change, not even in February. On the contrary, it became smoother and more phosphorescent and during the first nights of March it gave off a fragrance of roses.

Tobías smelled it. His blood attracted crabs and he spent half the night chasing them off his bed until the breeze rose up again and he was able to sleep. During his long moments of lying awake he learned how to distinguish all the changes in the air. So that when he got a smell of roses he didn't have to open up the door to know that it was a smell from the sea.

He got up late. Clotilde was starting a fire in the courtyard. The breeze was cool and all the stars were in place, but it was hard to count them down to the horizon because of the lights from the sea. After having his coffee, Tobías could still taste a trace of night on his palate.

'Something very strange happened last night,' he remembered.

Clotilde, of course, had not smelled it. She slept so heavily that she didn't even remember her dreams.

'It was a smell of roses,' Tobías said, 'and I'm sure it came from the sea.'

'I don't know what roses smell like,' said Clotilde.

She could have been right. The town was arid, with a hard soil furrowed by saltpeter, and only occasionally did someone bring a bouquet of flowers from outside to cast into the sea where they threw their dead.

'It's the smell that drowned man from Guacamayal had,' Tobías said.

'Well,' Clotilde said, smiling 'if it was a good smell, then you can be sure it didn't come from this sea.'

It really was a cruel sea. At certain times, when the nets brought in nothing but floating garbage, the streets of the town were still full of dead fish when the tide went out. Dynamite only brought the remains of old shipwrecks to the surface.

The few women left in town, like Clotilde, were boiling up with bitterness. And like her, there was old Jacob's wife, who got up earlier than usual that morning, put the house in order, and sat down to breakfast with a look of adversity.

'My last wish,' she said to her husband, 'is to be buried alive.'

She said it as if she were on her deathbed, but she was sitting across the table in a dining room with windows through which the bright March light came pouring in and spread throughout the house. Opposite her, calming his peaceful hunger, was old Jacob, a man who had loved her so much and for so long that he could no longer conceive of any suffering that didn't start with his wife.

'I want to die with the assurance that I'll be laid beneath the ground like proper people,' she went on. 'And the only way to be sure of it is to go around asking people to do me the blessed charity of burying me alive.'

'You don't have to ask anybody,' old Jacob said with the greatest of calm. 'I'll put you there myself.'

'Let's go, then,' she said, 'because I'm going to die before very long.'

Old Jacob looked her over carefully. Her eyes were the only thing still young. Her bones had become knotted up at the joints and she had the same look of a plowed field which, when it came right down to it, she had always had.

'You're in better shape than ever,' he told her.

'Last night I caught a smell of roses,' she sighed.

'Don't pay it any mind,' old Jacob said to assure her. 'Things like that are always happening to poor people like us.'

'Nothing of the sort,' she said. 'I've always prayed that I'd know enough ahead of time when death would come so I could die far away from this sea. A smell of roses in this town can only be a message from God.'

All that old Jacob could think of was to ask for a little time to put things in order. He'd heard tell that people don't die when they ought to but when they want to, and he was seriously worried by his wife's premonition. He even wondered whether, when the moment came, he'd be up to burying her alive.

At nine o'clock he opened the place where he used to have a store. He put two chairs and a small table with the checkerboard on it by the door and he spent all morning playing opponents who happened by. From his house he looked at the ruined town, the shambles of a town with the traces of former colors that had been nibbled away by the sun and a chunk of sea at the end of the street.

Before lunch, as always, he played with Don Máximo Gómez. Old Jacob couldn't imagine a more humane opponent than a man who had survived two civil wars intact and had only sacrificed an eye in the third. After losing one game on purpose, he held him back for another.

'Tell me one thing, Don Máximo,' he asked him then. 'Would you be capable of burying your wife alive?'

'Certainly,' Don Máximo Gómez answered. 'You can believe me when I say that my hand wouldn't even tremble.'

Old Jacob fell into a surprised silence. Then, after letting himself be despoiled of his best pieces, he sighed:

'Well, the way it looks, Petra is going to die.'

Don Máximo Gómez didn't change his expression. 'In that case,' he said, 'there's no reason to bury her alive.' He gobbled up two pieces and crowned a king. Then he fastened an eye wet with sad waters on his opponent.

'What's she got?'

'Last night,' old Jacob explained, 'she caught a smell of roses.'

'Then half the town is going to die,' Don Máximo Gómez said. 'That's all they've been talking about this morning.'

It was hard for old Jacob to lose again without offending him. He brought in the table and chairs, closed up the shop, and went about everywhere looking for someone who had caught the smell. In the end only Tobías was sure. So he asked him please to stop by his place, as if by chance, and tell his wife about it.

Tobías did as he was told. At four o'clock, all dressed up in his Sunday best, he appeared on the porch where the wife had spent all afternoon getting old Jacob's widower's outfit together.

He had come up so quietly that the woman was startled.

'Mercy,' she exclaimed. 'I thought it was the archangel Gabriel.'

'Well, you can see it's not,' Tobías said. 'It's only me and I've come to tell you something.'

She adjusted her glasses and went back to work.

'I know what it's all about,' she said.

'I bet you don't,' Tobías said.

'You caught the smell of roses last night.'

'How did you know?' Tobías asked in desolation.

'At my age,' the woman said, 'there's so much time left over for thinking that a person can become a regular prophet.'

Old Jacob, who had his ear pressed against the partition wall in the back of the store, stood up in shame.

'You see, woman,' he shouted through the wall. He made a turn and appeared on the porch. 'It wasn't what you thought it was after all.'

'This boy has been lying,' she said without raising her head. 'He didn't smell anything.'

'It was around eleven o'clock,' Tobías said. 'I was chasing crabs away.'

The woman finished mending a collar.

'Lies,' she insisted. 'Everybody knows you're a tricker.' She bit the thread with her teeth and looked at Tobías over her glasses.

'What I can't understand is why you went to the trouble to put Vaseline on your hair and shine your shoes just to come and be so disrespectful to me.'

From then on Tobías began to keep watch on the sea. He hung his hammock up on the porch by the yard and spent the night waiting, surprised by the things that go on in the world while people are asleep. For many nights he could hear the desperate scrawling of the crabs as they tried to claw-climb up the supports of the house, until so many nights went by that they got tired of trying. He came to know Clotilde's way of sleeping. He discovered how her fluty snores became more high-pitched as the heat grew more intense until they became one single languid note in the torpor of July.

At first Tobías kept watch on the sea the way people who know it well do, his gaze fixed on a single point of the horizon. He watched it change color. He watched it turn out its lights and become frothy and dirty and toss up its refuse-laden belches when great rainstorms agitated its digestion. Little by little he learned to keep watch the way people who know it better do, not even looking at it but unable to forget about it even in his sleep.

Old Jacob's wife died in August. She died in her sleep and they had to cast her, like everyone else, into a flowerless sea. Tobías kept on waiting. He had waited so long that it was becoming his way of being. One night, while he was dozing in his hammock, he realized that something in the air had changed. It was an intermittent wave, like the time a Japanese ship had jettisoned a cargo of rotten onions at the harbor mouth. Then the smell thickened and was motionless until dawn. Only when he had the feeling that he could pick it up in his hands and exhibit it did Tobías leap out of his hammock and go into Clotilde's room. He shook her several times.

'Here it is,' he told her.

Clotilde had to brush the smell away like a cobweb in order to get up. Then she fell back down on her tepid sheets.

'God curse it,' she said.

Tobías leaped toward the door, ran into the middle of the street, and began to shout. He shouted with all his might, took a deep breath and shouted again, and then there was a silence and he took a deeper breath, and the smell was still on the sea. But nobody answered. Then he went about knocking on doors from house to house, even on houses that had no owners, until his uproar got entwined with that of the dogs and he woke everybody up.

Many of them couldn't smell it. But others, especially the old ones, went down to enjoy it on the beach. It was a compact fragrance that left no chink for any odor of the past. Some, worn out from so much smelling, went back to their houses. Most of the people stayed to finish their night's sleep on the beach. By dawn the smell was so pure that it was a pity even to breathe it.

Tobías slept most of the day. Clotilde caught up with him at siesta time and they spent the afternoon frolicking in bed without even closing the door to the yard. First they did it like earthworms, then like rabbits, and finally like turtles, until the world grew sad and it was dark again. There was still a trace of roses in the air. Sometimes a wave of music reached the bedroom.

'It's coming from Catarino's,' Clotilde said. 'Someone must have come to town.'

Three men and a woman had come. Catarino thought that others might come later and he tried to fix his gramophone. Since he couldn't do it, he asked Pancho Aparecido, who did all kinds of things because he'd never owned anything, and besides, he had a box of tools and a pair of intelligent hands.

Catarino's place was a wooden building set apart and facing the sea. It had one large room with benches and small tables, and several bedrooms in the rear. While they watched Pancho Aparecido working, the three men and the woman drank in silence, sitting at the bar and yawning in turn.

The gramophone worked well after several tries. When they heard the music, distant but distinct, the people stopped chatting. They looked at one another and for a moment had nothing to say, for only then did they realize how old they had become since the last time they'd heard music.

Tobías found everybody still awake after nine o'clock. They were sitting in their doorways listening to Catarino's old records, with the same look of childish fatalism of people watching an eclipse. Every record reminded them of someone who had died, the taste of food after a long illness, or something they'd had to do the next day many years ago which never got done because they'd forgotten.

The music stopped around eleven o'clock. Many people went to bed, thinking it was going to rain because a dark cloud hung over the sea. But the cloud descended, floated for a while on the surface, and then sank into the water. Only the stars remained above. A short while later, the breeze went out from the town and came back with a smell of roses.

'Just what I told you, Jacob,' Don Máximo Gómez exclaimed. 'Here it is back with us again. I'm sure now that we're going to smell it every night.'

'God forbid,' old Jacob said. 'That smell is the only thing in life that's come too late for me.'

They'd been playing checkers in the empty store without paying any attention to the records. Their memories were so ancient that there weren't records old enough to stir them up.

'For my part, I don't believe much of anything about this,' Don Máximo Gómez said. 'After so many years of eating dust, with so many women wanting a little yard to plant flowers in, it's not strange that a person should end up smelling things like this and even thinking it's all true.'

'But we can smell it with our own noses,' old Jacob said.

'No matter,' said Don Máximo Gómez. 'During the war, when the revolution was already lost, we'd wanted a general so bad that we saw the Duke of Marlborough appear in flesh and blood. I saw him with my own eyes, Jacob.'

It was after midnight. When he was alone, old Jacob closed his store and took his lamp to the bedroom. Through the window, outlined against the glow of the sea, he saw the crag from which they threw their dead.

'Petra,' he called in a soft voice.

She couldn't hear him. At that moment she was floating along almost on the surface of the water beneath a radiant noonday sun on the Bay of Bengal. She'd lifted her head to look through the water, as through an illuminated showcase, at a huge ocean liner. But she couldn't see her husband, who at that moment on the other side of the world was starting to hear Catarino's gramophone again.

'Just think,' old Jacob said. 'Barely six months ago they thought you were crazy and now they're the ones making a festival out of the smell that brought on your death.'

He put out the light and got into bed. He wept slowly with that graceless little whimper old people have, but soon he fell asleep.

'I'd get away from this town if I could,' he sobbed as he tossed. 'I'd go straight to hell or anywhere else if I could only get twenty pesos together.'

From that night on and for several weeks, the smell remained on the sea. It impregnated the wood of the houses, the food, and the drinking water, and there was nowhere to escape the odor. A lot of people were startled to find it in the vapors of their own shit. The men and the woman who had come to Catarino's place left one Friday, but they were back on Saturday with a whole mob. More people arrived on Sunday. They were in and out of everywhere like ants, looking for something to eat and a place to sleep, until it got to be impossible to walk the streets.

More people came. The women who had left when the town died came back to Catarino's. They were fatter and wore heavier make-up, and they brought the latest records, which didn't remind anyone of anything. Some of the former inhabitants of the town returned. They'd gone off to get filthy rich somewhere else and they came back talking about their fortunes but wearing the same clothes they'd left with. Music and side shows arrived, wheels of chance, fortunetellers and gunmen and men with snakes coiled about their necks who were selling the elixir of eternal life. They kept on coming for many weeks, even after the first rains had come and the sea became rough and the smell disappeared.

A priest arrived among the last. He walked all over, eating bread dipped in light coffee, and little by little, he banned everything that had come before him: games of chance, the new music and the way it was danced, and even the recent custom of sleeping on the beach. One evening, at Melchor's house, he preached a sermon about the smell of the sea.

'Give thanks to heaven, my children,' he said, 'for this is the smell of God.'

Someone interrupted him.

'How can you tell, Father? You haven't smelled it yet.'

'The Holy Scriptures,' he said, 'are quite explicit in regard to this smell. We are living in a chosen village.'

Tobías went about back and forth in the festival like a sleepwalker. He took Clotilde to see what money was. They made believe they were betting enormous sums at roulette, and then they figured things up and felt extremely rich with all the money they could have won. But one night not just they, the whole multitude occupying the town, saw more money in one place than they could possibly have imagined.

That was the night Mr Herbert arrived. He appeared suddenly, set up a table in the middle of the street, and on top of the table placed two large trunks brimful with bank notes. There was so much money that no one noticed it at first, because they couldn't believe it was true. But when Mr Herbert started ringing a little bell, the people had to believe him, and they went over to listen.

'I'm the richest man in the world,' he said. 'I've got so much money I haven't got room to keep it any more. And besides, since my heart's so big that there's no room for it in my chest,

I have decided to travel the world over solving the problems of mankind.'

He was tall and ruddy. He spoke in a loud voice and without any pauses, and simultaneously he waved about a pair of lukewarm, languid hands that always looked as if they'd just been shaved. He spoke for fifteen minutes and rested. Then he rang the little bell and began to speak again. Halfway through his speech, someone in the crowd waved a hat and interrupted him.

'Come on, mister, don't talk so much and start handing out the money.'

'Not so fast,' Mr Herbert replied. 'Handing out money with no rhyme or reason, in addition to being an unfair way of doing things, doesn't make any sense at all.'

With his eyes he located the man who had interrupted him, and motioned him to come forward. The crowd let him through.

'On the other hand,' Mr Herbert went on, 'this impatient friend of ours is going to give us a chance to explain the most equitable system of the distribution of wealth.' He reached out a hand and helped him up.

'What's your name?'

'Patricio.'

'All right, Patricio,' Mr Herbert said. 'Just like everybody else, you've got some problem you haven't been able to solve for some time.'

Patricio took off his hat and confirmed it with a nod.

'What is it?'

'Well, my problem is this,' Patricio said. 'I haven't got any money.'

'How much do you need?'

'Forty-eight pesos.'

Mr Herbert gave an exclamation of triumph. 'Forty-eight pesos,' he repeated. The crowd accompanied him in clapping.

'Very well, Patricio,' Mr Herbert went on. 'Now, tell us one thing: what can you do?'

'Lots of things.'

'Decide on one,' Mr Herbert said. 'The thing you do best.'

'Well,' Patricio said, 'I can do birds.'

Applauding a second time, Mr Herbert turned to the crowd.

'So, then, ladies and gentlemen, our friend Patricio, who does an extraordinary job at imitating birds, is going to imitate forty-eight different birds and in that way he will solve the great problem of his life.'

To the startled silence of the crowd, Patricio then did his birds. Sometimes whistling, sometimes with his throat, he did all known birds and finished off the figure with others that no one was able to identify. When he was through, Mr Herbert called for a round of applause and gave him forty-eight pesos.

'And now,' he said, 'come up one by one. I'm going to be here until tomorrow at this time solving problems.'

Old Jacob learned about the commotion from the comments of people walking past his house. With each bit of news his heart grew bigger and bigger until he felt it burst.

'What do you think about this gringo?' he asked.

Don Máximo Gómez shrugged his shoulders. 'He must be a philanthropist.'

'If I could only do something,' old Jacob said, 'I could solve my little problem right now. It's nothing much: twenty pesos.'

'You play a good game of checkers,' Don Máximo Gómez said.

Old Jacob appeared not to have paid any attention to him, but when he was alone, he wrapped up the board and the box of checkers in a newspaper and went off to challenge Mr Herbert. He waited until midnight for his turn. Finally Mr Herbert had them pack up his trunks and said good-bye until the next morning.

He didn't go off to bed. He showed up at Catarino's place with the men who were carrying his trunks and the crowd followed him all the way there with their problems. Little by little, he went on solving them, and he solved so many that finally, in the store, the only ones left were the women and some men with their problems already solved. And in the back of the room there was a solitary woman fanning herself slowly with a cardboard advertisement.

'What about you?' Mr Herbert shouted at her. 'What's your problem?'

The woman stopped fanning herself.

'Don't try to get me mixed up in your fun, mister gringo,' she shouted across the room. 'I haven't got any kind of problem and I'm a whore because it comes out of my balls.'

Mr Herbert shrugged his shoulders. He went on drinking his cold beer beside the open trunks, waiting for other problems. He was sweating. A while later, a woman broke away from the group that was with her at the table and spoke to him in a low voice. She had a five-hundred-peso problem.

'How would you split that up?' Mr Herbert asked her.

'By five.'

'Just imagine,' Mr Herbert said. 'That's a hundred men.'

'It doesn't matter,' she said. 'If I can get all that money together they'll be the last hundred men of my life.'

He looked her over. She was quite young, fragile-boned, but her eyes showed a simple decision.

'All right,' Mr Herbert said. 'Go into your room and I'll start sending each one with his five pesos to you.'

He went to the street door and rang his little bell.

At seven o'clock in the morning Tobías found Catarino's place open. All the lights were out. Half asleep and puffed up with beer, Mr Herbert was controlling the entry of men into the girl's room.

Tobías went in too. The girl recognized him and was surprised to see him in her room.

'You too?'

'They told me to come in,' Tobías said. 'They gave me five pesos and told me not to take too long.'

She took the soaked sheet off the bed and asked Tobías to hold the other end. It was as heavy as canvas. They squeezed it, twisting it by the ends, until it got its natural weight back. They turned the mattress over and the sweat came out the other side. Tobías did things as best he could. Before leaving he put the five pesos on the pile of bills that was growing high beside the bed.

'Send everybody you can,' Mr Herbert suggested to him. 'Let's see if we can get this over with before noon.'

The girl opened the door a crack and asked for a cold beer. There were still several men waiting.

'How many left?' she asked.

'Sixty-three,' Mr Herbert answered.

Old Jacob followed him about all day with his checker-board. His turn came at nightfall and he laid out his problem and Mr Herbert accepted. They put two chairs and a small table on top of the big table in the middle of the street, and old Jacob made the first move. It was the last play he was able to premeditate. He lost.

'Forty pesos,' Mr Herbert said, 'and I'll give you a handicap of two moves.'

He won again. His hands barely touched the checkers. He played blindfolded, guessing his opponent's moves, and still won. The crowd grew tired of watching. When old Jacob decided to give up, he was in debt to the tune of five thousand seven hundred forty-two pesos and twenty-three cents.

He didn't change his expression. He jotted down the figure on a piece of paper he had in his pocket. Then he folded up the board, put the checkers in their box, and wrapped everything in the newspaper.

'Do with me what you will,' he said, 'but let me have these things. I promise you that I will spend the rest of my life getting all that money together.'

Mr Herbert looked at his watch.

'I'm terribly sorry,' he said. 'Your time will be up in twenty minutes.' He waited until he was sure that his opponent hadn't found the solution. 'Don't you have anything else to offer?'

'My honor.'

'I mean,' Mr Herbert explained, 'something that changes color when a brush daubed with paint is passed over it.'

'My house,' old Jacob said as if he were solving a riddle. 'It's not worth much, but it is a house.'

That was how Mr Herbert took possession of old Jacob's house. He also took possession of the houses and property of others who couldn't pay their debts, but he called for a week of music, fireworks, and acrobats and he took charge of the festivities himself.

It was a memorable week. Mr Herbert spoke of the miraculous destiny of the town and he even sketched out the city of the future, great glass buildings with dance floors on top. He showed it to the crowd. They looked in astonishment, trying to find themselves among the pedestrians painted in Mr Herbert's colors, but they were so well dressed that they couldn't recognize themselves. It pained them to be using him so much. They laughed at the urge they'd had to cry back in October and they kept on living in the midst of hope until Mr Herbert rang his little bell and said the party was over. Only then did he get some rest.

'You're going to die from that life you lead,' old Jacob said.

'I've got so much money that there's no reason for me to die,' Mr Herbert said.

He flopped onto his bed. He slept for days on end, snoring like a lion, and so many days went by that people grew tired of waiting on him. They had to dig crabs to eat. Catarino's new records got so old that no one could listen to them any more without tears, and he had to close his place up.

A long time after Mr Herbert had fallen asleep, the priest knocked on old Jacob's door. The house was locked from the inside. As the breathing of the man asleep had been using up the air, things had lost their weight and were beginning to float about.

'I want to have a word with him,' the priest said.

'You'll have to wait,' said old Jacob.

'I haven't got much time.'

'Have a seat, Father, and wait,' old Jacob repeated. 'And please talk to me in the meantime. It's been a long time since I've known what's been going on in the world.'

'People have all scattered,' the priest said. 'It won't be long before the town will be the same as it was before. That's the only thing that's new.'

'They'll come back when the sea smells of roses again,' old Jacob said.

'But meanwhile, we've got to sustain the illusions of those who stay with something,' the priest said. 'It's urgent that we start building the church.'

'That's why you've come to see Mr Herbert,' old Jacob said.

'That's right,' said the priest. 'Gringos are very charitable.'

'Wait a bit, then, Father,' old Jacob said. 'He might just wake up.'

They played checkers. It was a long and difficult game which lasted several days, but Mr Herbert didn't wake up.

The priest let himself be confused by desperation. He went all over with a copper plate asking for donations to build the church, but he didn't get very much. He was getting more and more diaphanous from so much begging, his bones were starting to fill with sounds, and one Sunday he rose two hands above the ground, but nobody noticed it. Then he packed his clothes in one suitcase and the money he had collected in another and said good-bye forever.

'The smell won't come back,' he said to those who tried to dissuade him. 'You've got to face up to the fact that the town has fallen into mortal sin.'

When Mr Herbert woke up the town was the same as it had been before. The rain had fermented the garbage the crowds had left in the streets and the soil was as arid and hard as a brick once more.

'I've been asleep a long time,' Mr Herbert said, yawning.

'Centuries,' said old Jacob.

'I'm starving to death.'

'So is everybody else,' old Jacob said. 'There's nothing to do but to go to the beach and dig for crabs.'

Tobías found him scratching in the sand, foaming at the mouth, and he was surprised to discover that when rich people were starving they looked so much like the poor. Mr Herbert didn't find enough crabs. At nightfall he invited Tobías to come look for something to eat in the depths of the sea.

'Listen,' Tobías warned him, 'only the dead know what's down inside there.'

'Scientists know too,' Mr Herbert said. 'Beneath the sea of the drowned there are turtles with exquisite meat on them. Get your clothes off and let's go.'

They went. At first they swam straight along and then down very deep to where the light of the sun stopped and then the light of the sea, and things were visible only in their own light. They passed by a submerged village with men and women on horseback turning about a musical kiosk. It was a splendid day and there were brightly colored flowers on the terraces.

'A Sunday sank at about eleven o'clock in the morning,' Mr Herbert said. 'It must have been some cataclysm.'

Tobías turned off toward the village, but Mr Herbert signaled him to keep going down.

'There are roses there,' Tobías said. 'I want Clotilde to know what they are.'

'You can come back another time at your leisure,' Mr Herbert said. 'Right now I'm dying of hunger.'

He went down like an octopus, with slow, slinky strokes of his arms. Tobías, who was trying hard not to lose sight of him, thought that it must be the way rich people swam. Little by little, they were leaving the sea of common catastrophes and entering the sea of the dead.

There were so many of them that Tobías thought that he'd never seen as many people on earth. They were floating motionless, face up, on different levels, and they all had the look of forgotten souls.

'They're very old dead,' Mr Herbert said. 'It's taken them centuries to reach this state of repose.'

Farther down, in the waters of the more recent dead, Mr Herbert stopped. Tobías caught up with him at the instant that a very young woman passed in front of them. She was floating on her side, her eyes open, followed by a current of flowers.

Mr Herbert put his finger to his lip and held it there until the last of the flowers went by.

'She's the most beautiful woman I've ever seen in all my life,' he said.

'She's old Jacob's wife,' Tobías said. 'She must be fifty years younger, but that's her. I'm sure of it.'

'She's done a lot of traveling,' Mr Herbert said. 'She's carrying behind her flowers from all the seas of the world.'

They reached bottom. Mr Herbert took a few turns over earth that looked like polished slate. Tobías followed him. Only when he became accustomed to the half light of the depths did he discover that the turtles were there. There were thousands of them, flattened out on the bottom, so motionless they looked petrified.

'They're alive,' Mr Herbert said, 'but they've been asleep for millions of years.'

He turned one over. With a soft touch he pushed it upward and the sleeping animal left his hands and continued drifting up. Tobías let it pass by. Then he looked toward the surface and saw the whole sea upside down.

'It's like a dream,' he said.

'For your own good,' Mr Herbert said, 'don't tell anyone about it. Just imagine the disorder there'd be in the world if people found out about these things.'

It was almost midnight when they got back to the village. They woke up Clotilde to boil some water. Mr Herbert butchered the turtle, but it took all three of them to chase and kill the heart a second time as it bounced out into the courtyard while they were cutting the creature up. They ate until they couldn't breathe any more.

'Well, Tobías,' Mr Herbert then said, 'we've got to face reality.'

'Of course.'

'And reality says,' Mr Herbert went on, 'that the smell will never come back.'

'It will come back.'

'It won't come back,' Clotilde put in, 'among other reasons because it never really came. It was you who got everybody all worked up.'

'You smelled it yourself,' Tobías said.

'I was half dazed that night,' Clotilde said. 'But right now I'm not sure about anything that has to do with this sea.'

'So I'll be on my way,' Mr Herbert said. 'And,' he added, speaking to both of them, 'you should leave too. There are too many things to do in the world for you to be starving in this town.'

He left. Tobías stayed in the yard counting the stars down to the horizon and he discovered that there were three more since last December. Clotilde called him from the bedroom, but he didn't pay any attention.

'Come here, you dummy,' Clotilde insisted. 'It's been years since we did it like rabbits.'

Tobías waited a long time. When he finally went in, she had fallen asleep. He half woke her, but she was so tired that they both got things mixed up and they were only able to do it like earthworms.

'You're acting like a boob,' Clotilde said grouchily. 'Try to think about something else.'

'I am thinking about something else.'

She wanted to know what it was and he decided to tell her on the condition that she wouldn't repeat it. Clotilde promised.

'There's a village at the bottom of the sea,' Tobías said, 'with little white houses with millions of flowers on the terraces.'

Clotilde raised her hands to her head.

'Oh, Tobías,' she exclaimed. 'Oh, Tobías, for the love of God, don't start up with those things again.'

Tobías didn't say anything else. He rolled over to the edge of the bed and tried to go to sleep. He couldn't until dawn, when the wind changed and the crabs left him in peace.

GABRIEL GARCÍA MÁRQUEZ

A celebration of one of the world's most loved writers. 16 beautiful new Penguin paperback editions, also available in ebook for the first time.

CHRONICLE OF A DEATH FORETOLD

COLLECTED STORIES

IN EVIL HOUR

INNOCENT ERENDIRA AND OTHER STORIES

LEAF STORM

LIVING TO TELL THE TALE

LOVE IN THE TIME OF CHOLERA

MEMORIES OF MY MELANCHOLY WHORES

NEWS OF A KIDNAPPING

NO ONE WRITES TO THE COLONEL

OF LOVE AND OTHER DEMONS

ONE HUNDRED YEARS OF SOLITUDE

STRANGE PILGRIMS

THE AUTUMN OF THE PATRIARCH

THE GENERAL IN HIS LABYRINTH

THE STORY OF A SHIPWRECKED SAILOR

He just wanted a decent book to read ...

Not too much to ask, is it? It was in 1935 when Allen Lane, Managing Director of Bodley Head Publishers, stood on a platform at Exeter railway station looking for something good to read on his journey back to London. His choice was limited to popular magazines and poor-quality paperbacks – the same choice faced every day by the vast majority of readers, few of whom could afford hardbacks. Lane's disappointment and subsequent anger at the range of books generally available led him to found a company – and change the world.

'We believed in the existence in this country of a vast reading public for intelligent books at a low price, and staked everything on it'
Sir Allen Lane, 1902–1970, founder of Penguin Books

The quality paperback had arrived – and not just in bookshops. Lane was adamant that his Penguins should appear in chain stores and tobacconists, and should cost no more than a packet of cigarettes.

Reading habits (and cigarette prices) have changed since 1935, but Penguin still believes in publishing the best books for everybody to enjoy. We still believe that good design costs no more than bad design, and we still believe that quality books published passionately and responsibly make the world a better place.

So wherever you see the little bird – whether it's on a piece of prize-winning literary fiction or a celebrity autobiography, political tour de force or historical masterpiece, a serial-killer thriller, reference book, world classic or a piece of pure escapism – you can bet that it represents the very best that the genre has to offer.

Whatever you like to read – trust Penguin.